Is It True About Mom?

Elizabeth took a deep breath. "Mom, did you and Dad fall in love at first sight?"

"How did you meet?" Jessica asked. "Was it romantic?"

"Or a complete surprise, like a chance encounter in an airport?" Elizabeth added.

Mrs. Wakefield sat up as if to answer, but then she said, "I'm sorry. I am so tired and it's a long story. Could you ask me again tomorrow? Good night, girls."

"Mom! Aren't you even going to say good night to Dad?" Jessica cried after her.

"Oh, I almost forgot he was here," Mrs. Wakefield murmured. She stuck her head into the den and called, "Good night. I'm going right up to bed." Mr. Wakefield glanced up from the basketball game on TV and blew his wife a kiss.

Jessica and Elizabeth watched with a growing sense of dread as their mom left them.

"Did you hear that? She almost forgot Dad was here!" Jessica said.

"And she wasn't excited about telling us how they fell in love, either," Elizabeth whispered.

"That's because she's in love with somebody else!" Jessica whispered back. "We've got to do something before it's too late!"

Bantam Skylark Books in the SWEET VALLEY TWINS series
Ask your bookseller for the books you have missed

#1 BEST FRIENDS
#2 TEACHER'S PET
#3 THE HAUNTED HOUSE
#4 CHOOSING SIDES
#5 SNEAKING OUT
#6 THE NEW GIRL
#7 THREE'S A CROWD
#8 FIRST PLACE
#9 AGAINST THE RULES
#10 ONE OF THE GANG
#11 BURIED TREASURE
#12 KEEPING SECRETS
#13 STRETCHING THE TRUTH
#14 TUG OF WAR
#15 THE OLDER BOY
#16 SECOND BEST
#17 BOYS AGAINST GIRLS
#18 CENTER OF ATTENTION
#19 THE BULLY
#20 PLAYING HOOKY
#21 LEFT BEHIND
#22 OUT OF PLACE
#23 CLAIM TO FAME
#24 JUMPING TO CONCLUSIONS

Sweet Valley Twins Super Editions

#1 THE CLASS TRIP
#2 HOLIDAY MISCHIEF

SWEET VALLEY TWINS

Jumping to Conclusions

Written by
Jamie Suzanne

Created by
FRANCINE PASCAL

A BANTAM SKYLARK BOOK®
TORONTO · NEW YORK · LONDON · SYDNEY · AUCKLAND

RL 4, 008–012

JUMPING TO CONCLUSIONS
A Bantam Skylark Book / November 1988

*Skylark Books is a registered trademark of Bantam Books,
a division of Bantam Doubleday Dell Publishing Group, Inc.
Registered in U.S. Patent and Trademark Office and elsewhere.*

*Sweet Valley High® and Sweet Valley Twins are
trademarks of Francine Pascal.*

Conceived by Francine Pascal.

*Produced by Daniel Weiss Associates, Inc.,
27 West 20th Street, New York, NY 10011*

Cover art by James Mathewuse.

To Jake Michael Nardi

One

◇

"The decorations look beautiful!" Elizabeth Wakefield said, clapping her hands in delight as she surveyed the family's living room. Pink-and-white streamers were looped from wall to wall above her head. Through the picture window she could see the sun just beginning to set over Sweet Valley, California. "What a perfect night for a party!" she exclaimed.

Elizabeth and her twin sister, Jessica, had spent the entire afternoon decorating and cooking. Today was their parents' sixteenth wedding anniversary and it had been Jessica's idea to have a special party to celebrate. For two weeks the twins had thought of nothing but their big secret.

"I hope they're surprised," Jessica called from

the kitchen. "I'm sure they will be," Elizabeth called back as she straightened the "Happy Anniversary, Mom and Dad!" banner stretched across the entryway. "I haven't breathed a word to anyone."

"This is going to be great," Jessica declared as she entered the dining room. She carried a large bouquet in her hands. The sisters had picked sixteen yellow roses from their mother's rose garden, then carefully mixed them with wildflowers.

As they set the flowers on the sideboard, they both noticed their reflection in the mirror on the wall. They were identical in almost every way. Their blue-green eyes were the color of the Pacific Ocean and their shiny blond hair fell in waves over their shoulders. Even the dimples in their left cheeks matched when they smiled.

Only their family and closest friends could tell the girls apart, and those who knew them best knew that their similarities were only skin-deep. When it came to their personalities, they couldn't have been more different.

Elizabeth loved nothing more than to indulge in a good mystery, preferably one by Amanda Howard, her favorite writer. In addition, Elizabeth worked hard in school and was proud to be a member of the staff of *The Sweet Valley Sixers*, the sixth-grade paper.

Jessica, on the other hand, loved clothes and boys and her after-school activities, especially being a member of the Unicorns, an exclusive all-girls club at Sweet Valley Middle School. And it was just like Jessica to think that no party ever really got started until she entered the room. But, in spite of all their differences, the twins were still the best of friends.

"You know," Jessica said, "it feels like ages since our family has been together. Sometimes I feel like we should schedule family meetings, just to remind us all what we look like."

Elizabeth laughed. "It hasn't been that bad, Jess."

"Well, ever since Dad started that big case, we hardly see him," Jessica pointed out. Their father was a successful lawyer in Sweet Valley, and his hours could be very demanding.

"That's true," Elizabeth said.

"And what about Steven?" Jessica put her hands on her hips. "He's never home."

"I know," Elizabeth agreed. "He's always at basketball practice."

"Which is fine with me," Jessica added with a smile.

Since he had begun his freshman year at Sweet Valley High, their brother had been harder to live with than ever. Even Elizabeth found his constant bragging about being older and wiser a little irritating.

"But it's Mom who's been gone the most," Jessica said, her voice suddenly turning serious.

Elizabeth nodded. "She's been spending a lot of time working with her clients." Mrs. Wakefield worked part-time as an interior decorator but lately it seemed as if it was full-time.

"She's also been dining with strange men," Jessica added.

"Now, Jessica," Elizabeth scolded. "Be fair. You saw her in a restaurant with a man *once*—and you never even asked her about it."

Jessica had seen their mother having lunch with a man whom she didn't recognize a few days earlier and had been brooding about it ever since. Elizabeth guessed that, similar to the time when Mrs. Wakefield had been ill, Jessica's overactive imagination was hard at work again.

"Well, she *has* been gone a lot," Jessica insisted, "and if it weren't for you and me running things, this house would be a mess."

Elizabeth grinned. It was just like Jessica to take credit for the extra chores they had been asked to do—chores which Elizabeth usually wound up doing.

"Well, what do you think?" Jessica pointed to a platter full of sandwiches on the sideboard.

"They served these at our last Unicorn party and they were a big hit."

Elizabeth picked up one of the sandwiches and took a bite. "Hey! These are delicious."

"Don't eat them all!" Jessica said, swatting playfully at her sister's hand. "Save some for Mom and Dad."

"Did you call about the cake?" Elizabeth asked.

"Steven was supposed to pick it up from the bakery but he's late—as usual."

"Don't panic. Mom and Dad aren't supposed to be back for another half an hour."

"Half an hour!" Jessica raced toward the kitchen. "We'll never make it in time."

The front door slammed and Steven called from the hallway, "You can start the party now. I'm here."

"Very funny!" Jessica shouted, walking back into the kitchen. "Bring that cake in here, quickly."

Elizabeth carefully placed four long-stemmed roses around two tiny figures that stood in the center of the dining room table. They were the figures that had been on Mr. and Mrs. Wakefield's wedding cake sixteen years ago.

Steven strolled into the dining room, and looked over Elizabeth's shoulder. "Wow, where did you find those?" he asked.

"In Mom's trunk."

Steven stared at the tiny man in his formal tuxedo and the tiny woman in her frilly wedding dress and shook his head. "Boy, why would anyone want to dress up like that!"

"Because it's romantic," Jessica said, coming up behind them. "I can just see them on their wedding day."

Elizabeth sighed. "I'll bet Mom looked beautiful!"

"Cut it out, you two," Steven said, making a face and groaning. Then he caught sight of the tray on the sideboard. "Hey, sandwiches!"

"Don't you dare, Steven Wakefield!" Jessica leapt in front of him. "Those are for the party."

"But I'm dying of hunger," he pleaded.

"You'll have some later." Elizabeth cut in.

Steven reluctantly backed off.

"We'd better do a last minute check to make sure everything is ready," Elizabeth told her sister.

"The hors d'oeuvres are done. I have the casserole ready to pop in the oven," Jessica said, counting the items on her fingers. "The cake is here and—"

"Did you hear that?" Steven rushed to the window. "It sounded like a car," Elizabeth whispered.

Jessica raced to the living room and peered through the drapes. "It's them!" she shouted. "Hurry, turn off the lights."

Elizabeth flicked the switch and the three of them scrambled behind the couch to hide.

"Ouch!" Jessica cried as Steven stepped on her foot. "Steven, watch where you're going."

"*You* watch where—"

"Shhhh!" Elizabeth hissed.

The three held their breath and listened for the sound of the key in the lock. The front door creaked open.

"Hello?" It was their mother's voice. "Anybody here?" When there was no response, she said, "That's strange, the children should all be home by now."

Then their father's voice rumbled in the darkened room. "I thought I saw a light on when we pulled into the driveway."

Jessica started giggling. Steven jabbed her to make her stop, but within seconds Elizabeth was laughing as hard as her sister.

"Ready?" Steven whispered hoarsely. "One, two, three—"

"SURPRISE!" they all shouted.

"What's all this about?" their father asked as the light flicked on. He looked over at his wife, who was equally confused.

"I don't know," she replied. "Kids, is this a joke?"

"A joke? How can you ask that, Mom? It's for your anniversary," Jessica explained. "Don't you remember?"

"Anniversary?" Their parents clapped their hands to their foreheads. "Oh, no!" they echoed in unison.

"Did you both forget?" Elizabeth asked in amazement.

"How *could* you?" Jessica couldn't hide the disappointment in her voice.

"I guess we've been kind of busy," Mr. Wakefield replied, lifting his hands in a helpless gesture.

Mrs. Wakefield sighed dramatically. "We knew the romance couldn't last forever."

"Don't say that!" Jessica cried out. "It's not funny."

Mr. Wakefield looked at Jessica sharply. "It's just a joke, Jessica."

"Does this mean we can't eat the cake and sandwiches?" Steven asked.

Jessica turned to him, her eyes blazing. "Is your stomach all you can ever think of?"

"Well . . . sometimes."

Elizabeth decided this was a good moment to

interject. "How do you like the decorations? It was Jessica's idea to give you a party."

Jessica nodded but said nothing. Her stomach was starting to feel queasy. *They haven't kissed, or hugged, or anything,* she thought. *Don't they care anymore?* Suddenly, she remembered seeing her mother with that other man.

"Jessica?"

Jessica looked up to see Elizabeth waving at her. "What?"

Elizabeth made eating motions with her hand and pointed toward the kitchen.

"Oh. Right." Jessica decided just to concentrate on the anniversary party for now.

That night as Elizabeth was getting ready for bed, she heard a soft knock at her door.

"Lizzie, it's me," Jessica whispered. "I need to talk to you."

"What's the matter, Jess?" Elizabeth asked as her sister entered her room.

"It's Mom and Dad," Jessica whispered. "I'm really worried."

"Just because they forgot their anniversary?"

Jessica sat on the edge of the bed. "People don't forget an important event like that unless there's something really wrong."

"They've both been awfully busy recently." Elizabeth sat down next to her sister.

"I know. And that's another thing." Jessica whispered, "Have you noticed they hardly go out together anymore?"

"Look," Elizabeth said patiently. "Dad has that big case right now and Mom's had to spend more time on the job than usual. It's not going to be this way forever."

"Well, I'm not so sure," Jessica said.

"What's that supposed to mean?"

"Maybe it's like Mom said, the romance is all gone. Lizzie, what if they're just pretending for our sakes?"

"Now you're being silly." Elizabeth stood up. "I'm really tired. Let's get some sleep. I'm sure everything will look better in the morning."

"I hope you're right." Jessica hugged her sister and trudged back to her room.

As she drifted off to sleep she couldn't help thinking, *People who love each other just don't forget their anniversary.*

Two

◇

At lunchtime on Monday Amy Sutton looked up from her tray and declared, "Why did the Hairnet do this to us!" Everyone at Sweet Valley Middle School called Mrs. Arnette, the social studies teacher, "the Hairnet" because she always wore a brown net over her tight bun. Amy picked up a handful of potato chips and stuffed a few into her mouth. "Can you believe it? A big report due in two weeks."

Elizabeth smiled at her best friend. They had decided to meet at lunch to think up ideas for their new social studies project. So far they had gotten nowhere.

"Amy, it's not that bad," Elizabeth said. "With three of us working on it, it should be easy."

"A report for Mrs. Arnette is never easy," Pamela Jacobson announced as she slid her lunch tray onto the table and sat down next to Elizabeth.

Pamela had only started attending Sweet Valley Middle School a few months earlier, but she had quickly become good friends with Elizabeth and Amy. She had eagerly volunteered to be in their group working on the report.

"I'm glad you're here, Pamela." Elizabeth smiled at the pale brunette. "Tell Amy that our Living History report will be fun."

Pamela turned toward Amy and with a serious expression repeated Elizabeth's words. "Our Living History report will be fun."

Elizabeth laughed and gave Pamela a playful punch. "You're just as bad as Amy!"

Amy sighed. "I can't help thinking that history's just a lot of boring dates. Every time Mrs. Arnette starts to write one on the blackboard . . ." She stopped talking and dropped her head onto the table, letting out a loud snore. Elizabeth and Pamela couldn't resist a giggle.

Pamela opened her carton of milk and put her straw in it. "Why don't we go over the assignment again to see how much work we have to do?"

"Good idea." Elizabeth flipped open her notebook. "First we have to find someone in Sweet Valley to interview."

"Right." Amy took a huge bite of her grilled cheese sandwich and mumbled, "Then we ask them questions."

"Then we go to the library and do a little research on the era or subject they discuss," Elizabeth said.

"And finally, we put it all together and present the report to the class," Pamela finished.

Elizabeth smiled at her friends. "It could be a lot of fun."

Amy groaned. "Or it could be a lot of work. Besides, who do we know who's interesting? I can't think of anyone."

Elizabeth sighed. "I wish we could do a report about romance—maybe something about love and adventure." Elizabeth turned to Pamela. "How did your parents meet?"

Pamela began to answer, then paused, a surprised look on her face. "Gee, I don't know."

"Do you know how your mom and dad fell in love?" Elizabeth asked Amy.

She shook her head slowly. "I never asked."

"Me, neither," Elizabeth said.

"I guess I never really thought about it," Amy added. "I think of my parents as always having been married. It's hard to imagine them apart."

Amy lowered her voice dramatically. "I've got it," she declared. ". . . Mom and Dad are in a crowded airport. They bump into each other accidentally and Mom's suitcase falls on the ground. Dad reaches down to pick it up, their eyes meet—it's *fate!*"

"Oooh!" Elizabeth let out a squeal of delight. "This is just like a romance novel. Let's do our project on our own parents."

"What a great idea!" Pamela clapped her hands together.

"We could call it 'Sweet Valley Sweethearts,'" Elizabeth added. Amy nodded enthusiastically. "This could be a really interesting report."

"Don't forget, we still have to find other stories to go along with the interviews," Pamela reminded them.

"We could go to the library and each do a report on romance. You know, famous romantic couples in history," Elizabeth said excitedly.

"And literature," Amy added.

"And we could end our report with a love poem," Pamela concluded.

"Then it's settled." Elizabeth shut her notebook. "We'll each interview our parents and find out how they met."

"This is going to be great," Amy declared. "I never thought I'd get excited about a project for the Hairnet."

Amy and Pamela chattered on about their

project while Elizabeth sat quietly, thinking about her parents.

This project will be just the thing to put the romance back in their lives. Elizabeth couldn't wait to get home and tell Jessica about her plan.

Jessica checked her watch for the fifteenth time. School had been out for over an hour and there was still no sign of Elizabeth. Finally she spotted her sister coming down their street and she ran to meet her.

"Lizzie, I have to talk to you!"

"What's the matter?" Elizabeth asked.

Jessica motioned for Elizabeth to follow her around the side of the house to the old pine tree. The twins used to go there to share secrets when they were younger and they had called it their "thinking seat."

Elizabeth frowned. Whatever Jessica wanted to talk about must be pretty serious because only Elizabeth still went there when she had a problem to think through.

"Jessica," she pleaded. "Please tell me what's wrong."

"It's Mom," Jessica whispered. "I heard her on the phone, talking to someone."

"So? It's probably just a client calling about a

job." Mrs. Wakefield's clients were always calling her at home.

"I couldn't really hear what they were saying because Mom finished the call in the bedroom and shut the door." Jessica crossed her arms. "But I'll tell you this—she was sure doing a lot of laughing for a business call."

"Jessica, you're being silly."

"And that's not all." Jessica lowered her voice. "The phone rang again five minutes later and it was the same man."

"How do you know it was a man?"

"I listened on the extension."

"Jessica!" Elizabeth was shocked. "That's spying. How could you?"

"I had to!" Jessica's blue-green eyes glistened with tears. "Oh, Lizzie, don't you see? First Mom is away half the time. Then she forgets her wedding anniversary. And now she's flirting with a strange man on the phone—"

"What do you mean, flirting? Mom wouldn't—"

"Right after Mom hung up she rushed out of the house." Jessica paced back and forth on the grass in front of the tree. "She's going to leave us, I just know it. She'll run off with some rich Arab. He'll promise her all the things Dad can't afford, and then we'll never see her again!"

"You're being ridiculous," Elizabeth cut in. "Where in the world did you come up with a story like that?"

"I saw it on a late-night movie once," Jessica replied matter-of-factly. "It was called *The Desert Siren* and it was based on a true story. Things like this happen *all* the time, Lizzie."

"Look, Jessica," Elizabeth interrupted, "there's a simple way to find out if you're right. Let's just ask Mom about the call when she gets home."

"She won't admit she's fallen in love just like that!"

"Mom has *not* fallen in love," Elizabeth declared. "With a rich Arab or anyone else!"

Jessica opened her mouth to protest but Elizabeth was already marching toward their back door. "I just hope you're right," Jessica whispered under her breath.

When they came through the door, Mrs. Wakefield was standing at the kitchen counter, removing a cardboard box from a brown paper bag. Her face was flushed with excitement and she turned to greet her daughters with a smile.

"There you both are! Sorry I'm late but I had to go back to the office."

Jessica pinched Elizabeth's arm.

"Since we're stuck with eating TV dinners tonight," Mrs. Wakefield said, "I thought a special surprise was in order."

"What sort of surprise?" Elizabeth asked, rubbing her bruised arm.

"Blueberry cheesecake!" Mrs. Wakefield flipped open the lid of the box to reveal the luscious dessert inside.

Elizabeth and Jessica stared solemnly at their mother.

"Oh, I know you're disappointed that I haven't been able to cook a proper dinner lately," their mother said. "But you'll have to bear with me for a while. I started working on a new account for a man from L.A."

Elizabeth felt a nudge from Jessica but tried to ignore it.

"He's opening a new office here in Sweet Valley and he wants me to decorate it! It's one of the biggest accounts we've ever had and I'm in charge of the whole thing." She grinned proudly. "Not bad, huh?"

"What's this guy like?" Jessica demanded. Elizabeth winced at the suspicious tone in her sister's voice. Their mother didn't seem to notice but rattled on gaily.

"Well, for one thing, he's very wealthy."

This time the nudge in her side was so sharp, Elizabeth gasped with pain. She spun around to face Jessica, who glared back at her as if to say, "I told you so!"

"He's got a huge home in Beverly Hills," their mother continued, as she popped some frozen dinners into the oven. "But he's hardly ever there. Most of the time he calls in from his private jet."

Mrs. Wakefield reached into her briefcase and pulled out a magazine. "Here's a picture of his house. It was the featured home in this month's issue of *Designer's Monthly*."

The twins stared at the photograph in awe. The mansion was three stories high and looked like a castle. Off in the distance they could see a pool and tennis courts. A big silver limousine sat in the driveway with a chauffeur standing at attention beside it.

"Wow." Jessica's stomach did flip-flops.

"What's his name?" Elizabeth asked.

"Francis Howard," Mrs. Wakefield replied. "Everyone calls him Frank, though. He's a very nice man."

"What's he look like, Mom?" Jessica asked in a shaky voice.

Their mother paused for a moment, then shrugged. "He's pretty normal-looking, I guess. He has a nice smile."

The phone rang suddenly and both girls jumped at the sound. Elizabeth answered it.

"Hello." A deep voice rumbled in her ear. "May I speak with Alice—I mean, Mrs. Wakefield?"

"Just a minute, please," Elizabeth said. She covered the mouthpiece with her palm and said, "Mom, it's for you."

"Thanks, honey." Mrs. Wakefield took the receiver from her and said, "Hello? Oh, hi, Frank. Just a minute. Let me go into the other room." She handed the phone back to Elizabeth. "Hang that up for me, OK?"

She walked briskly out of the kitchen and into their father's study. "I've got it!" she called out. Then they heard her voice fade away as the door to the study shut behind her.

Elizabeth stared at her sister. Jessica's lower lip was trembling. "*Now* do you believe me?" Jessica said sadly.

Three

◇

"I made up a list of sample questions for us to use in our interviews," Elizabeth announced, handing Pamela and Amy each a neatly printed copy from her binder. "What do you think?"

The three girls had gone to Pamela's house after school on Wednesday to plan the next step for the Living History project. They had made themselves comfortable in the den, and were now discussing the finer points.

"Oh, this is great, Liz!" Pamela said as she passed around sodas and chips. "I thought maybe we could interview my mom this afternoon."

"Good idea." Elizabeth took a sip of her

drink. "That will give us a chance to practice some interview techniques."

"I hope you guys don't mind," Amy said sheepishly, "but I talked to my parents last night. I just couldn't wait to find out how they met and fell in love."

"That's OK." Elizabeth smiled at her friend. "Did you take a lot of notes?"

"No, but I have every detail memorized." Amy, who was sitting on the floor, raised herself up on her knees. Her voice became hushed and excited as she began to tell her story.

"When my parents were both seniors in high school, they got summer jobs working at an amusement park. Dad ran the loop-the-loop ride and Mom took tickets at the gate."

"Did they know each other from school?" Pamela interrupted.

Amy shook her head. "No, Dad went to Crestview High. They'd never even seen each other before the Fourth of July. Anyway, that night, after the park was closed to the public, the owners kept the rides running for the employees."

"Sounds like fun," Elizabeth said, settling back on the couch.

"So Mom decided she'd ride the Ferris wheel and—"

"And that's where they met?" Pamela asked eagerly.

"Yes, but first—"

"I thought you said your dad ran the loop-the-loop," Elizabeth cut in.

"He did but he decided to go for a ride on the Ferris wheel, too." Amy sighed with exasperation. "But wait, I haven't even gotten to the good part yet.

"So there they were, all standing in line, waiting to get on the Ferris wheel. Then the man who ran the ride put Mom and Dad together in the same chair."

Elizabeth's eyes grew bigger with anticipation.

"Now here's the best part." Amy took a long sip of her soda and then whispered, "The Ferris wheel got stuck when the two of them were at the very top."

"Oooh, how scary!" Pamela blurted out.

"They were up there for almost an hour!" Amy continued.

"I'd have died of fright," Elizabeth said.

"Mom told me she was absolutely petrified and started to get hysterical. Dad had to calm her down by explaining how the ride worked and what the problem might be. He talked her right out of being scared. Then Mom noticed the full moon above them." Amy beamed happily. "By the time they got back down to the bottom, they were in love."

Both Pamela and Elizabeth sighed. "How romantic!" Elizabeth said.

Amy leaned back on her elbows. "Yes, isn't it a great story?"

All three girls sat silently, dreamily imagining the couple in the moonlight, perched high up on the top of the Ferris wheel.

"Elizabeth, have you asked your parents how they met?" Amy asked.

Elizabeth felt her cheeks turn pink, thinking of how little time her parents spent together these days. "Uh, n-no. I haven't asked, yet. They've both been really busy with their work, you know."

Elizabeth was relieved that neither of her friends seemed to notice how uncomfortable she was.

"Well, I can't wait to hear about it next time," Pamela said enthusiastically.

"Hello, girls." Mrs. Jacobson stood at the door to the den, holding a tray in her hands. "I thought you might need some healthy snacks to get you through your research."

"Thanks, Mom," Pamela said, as her mother

placed a tray of celery sticks, carrots, and dip on the coffee table.

"Have you girls been working hard?" Mrs. Jacobson asked as she passed around napkins. "Pamela told me all about your Living History project. I think it's a wonderful idea."

Elizabeth couldn't help feeling a pang of jealousy. It just didn't seem like there was any time, lately, when she could sit down and talk to her mother.

"Mom," Pamela said, "we thought we'd try out our interview techniques on you. Is that all right?"

"Sure." Mrs. Jacobson laughed and took a seat on the couch. "Fire away."

Pamela opened her notebook and reached for a pencil. "How did you and Dad meet?"

"And when did you fall in love?" Amy chimed in.

"Unless, of course, they happened at the same time," Elizabeth added, getting back into the spirit of things.

"Well, not exactly," Mrs. Jacobson replied slowly.

"You mean, it wasn't love at first sight?" Pamela sounded disappointed.

"No," Mrs. Jacobson replied with a laugh. "It was more like third sight."

"Oh," Pamela made a note on her pad, "what does that mean, Mom?"

"You see, the first time I met Dr. Jacobson," Pamela's mother explained, "I was in such pain from my sprained ankle that I hardly noticed how handsome he was."

"How'd you sprain your ankle?" Elizabeth asked.

"Playing volleyball with my sorority team. They rushed me to the emergency room and he was the doctor who wrapped my ankle. That was the first time I saw him. When I had to go back to the hospital for a follow-up examination, I was in better spirits and I noticed his good looks. But I wasn't sure if he was interested in me until he scheduled a house call for my sprained ankle." Mrs. Jacobson smiled at the memory. "He paid me a visit at the sorority house and the next thing I knew, we were engaged."

Elizabeth sighed wistfully. "I hope the next time I sprain my ankle, a handsome doctor rescues me and we fall in love, just like that."

"Thanks, Mom," Pamela said, giving her mother a big hug. "That was terrific!"

"Well, I'll leave you girls alone," Mrs. Jacobson said. "I'm sure you've got lots more to do."

After she had left the room, Elizabeth sat quietly, nibbling a carrot stick. "I hope my parents' story is half as romantic as yours both are."

"It will be," Amy said. "Your parents are the perfect couple. They're so much in love."

Elizabeth didn't respond. *Maybe they're just pretending to be in love, for our sake,* she thought. She shook her head to chase the thought away.

"You're right," she said, smiling bravely. "They *are* the perfect couple."

That afternoon Jessica walked home after school with Lila Fowler, a fellow Unicorn and one of her best friends. Lila was one of the prettiest girls in the sixth grade and she knew it. She dressed only in the best and latest fashions. Sometimes Jessica felt envious of her friend, whose father was very wealthy and gave her anything she wanted.

As they strolled along, the two Unicorns chatted about clothes, boys, and the latest gossip. Lila did most of the talking, but Jessica was having a hard time keeping her mind on the conversation.

"So I said to her, 'Caroline, do you really think I care?'" Lila laughed with satisfaction as they rounded the corner to the Wakefield home. "Oh, Jessica, you should have seen her face! She looked like a prune."

Jessica froze suddenly and stared straight ahead.

"Jessica? Are you listening to me?" Lila demanded, tossing her perfectly combed hair over one shoulder.

Jessica didn't reply. She was too busy staring at the silver limousine that was parked in front of her house. The windows were made of dark glass so you couldn't see inside. The door opened and a man stepped out onto the sidewalk.

"Who's that?" Lila whispered. Jessica shook her head in awe. He was without a doubt the most distinguished-looking man she had ever seen. Tall and ruggedly built, he was dressed in an elegant suit. He walked briskly up to the front entrance and slipped a skinny cardboard tube between the screen and the door. As he turned around to walk back to the car, the girls got a closer look at his tanned face.

"He looks like a movie star," Jessica exclaimed.

"I know who that is!" Lila hissed.

"Who?"

"Frank Howard, the millionaire."

Jessica felt like she'd been hit in the stomach. "No!"

"Yes," Lila continued, her voice trembling with excitement. "I read about him in *Faces* magazine. Women go crazy over him but he's never gotten married."

The man got back into the limousine and the car pulled away from the curb. The girls watched in silence as the sleek car disappeared around the corner.

A sudden breeze rustled the leaves and Jessica shivered. She thought to herself miserably, *Mom will never be able to resist a man like Frank Howard.*

Four

◇

That evening, Jessica and Elizabeth entered the kitchen with a chorus of questions.

"What's for dinner?" Elizabeth asked.

"Where's Mom?" Jessica demanded.

Mr. Wakefield was standing by the counter, leafing through the phone book. "You're just the pair I need to see," he said. "Your mom just called to say she won't be home for dinner."

"Not again!" Jessica exclaimed.

"Where is she?" Elizabeth asked.

"She had to work late," her father replied. "So dinner is up to me. What do you say we send out for pizza and watch a little TV?"

"Sounds great to me," Steven announced from the refrigerator. He had poured himself a huge glass of milk and was balancing a plate piled high with cookies. "I'm starved."

"Steven!" Jessica snapped. "How can you think of eating at a time like this?"

He stared at her blankly. "What are you talking about? It's dinnertime. What else should I be thinking about?"

Jessica didn't answer but stormed past him into the hall.

"What's with her?" Steven asked.

Elizabeth shook her head and shrugged. Steven turned his attention back to Mr. Wakefield. "Hurry up and order, Dad. The basketball game is about to start."

"Orders, anyone?" Mr. Wakefield asked. "What would you like on the pizza?"

"Anything's fine with me, Dad," Elizabeth said quietly.

"Pepperoni. Or sausage," Steven declared as he walked into the family room to turn on the television. "Maybe both," he shouted back as an afterthought.

Elizabeth stepped into the hallway and leaned against the wall. Behind her she heard her dad's voice call out from the kitchen.

"Set your timers, everybody! They have exactly thirty minutes to get it to us piping hot, or else!"

*He sounds awfully cheerful for a man whose wife
has told him she's working late. Too cheerful as a matter
of fact. Maybe even glad that Mom isn't with us,* Elizabeth thought.

"Elizabeth." She looked up to see Jessica behind the banister, gesturing for her to come closer.

"What?"

"I think Mom is out with Mr. Howard."

"So what if she is?"

Jessica looked deeply into her sister's eyes. "I'm starting to get really worried."

"Jessica!" Elizabeth crossed her arms impatiently. "Mom told us all about Mr. Howard yesterday. He's just a rich client from Beverly Hills. That's all."

"Oh, yeah?" Jessica stuck out her lip stubbornly. "Mom left out one very important fact."

"What?"

"Mr. Howard is gorgeous!"

"How do you know?"

"I happened to be coming home this afternoon just as he stopped by to drop off some stuff for Mom." Jessica clutched her twin's arm. "Lizzie, he looks just like a movie star!"

"So?" Elizabeth blinked at her sister.

Jessica threw her hands in the air. "So why did she tell us Mr. Howard was just a normal-looking guy? Maybe she was trying to hide the fact that she was in love with him."

Elizabeth folded her arms in front of her and stared at her sister. "That's an awful thing to say!"

"Are you just going to stand there while some millionaire breaks up our parents' marriage and takes Mom off to his mansion?"

"No," Elizabeth said, marching past her sister on the stairs. "I'm going to talk to Mom tonight."

"*If* she comes home," Jessica called after her. "She could be at some restaurant with Mr. Howard right now, eating dinner by candlelight and planning how they're going to run off together."

"Jessica," Elizabeth cried out. "Those things only happen in the movies."

Her sister looked unconvinced.

"Besides," Elizabeth added, "you're forgetting Dad."

"What about him?"

"He'd never let something like that happen."

"That's just it, Elizabeth," Jessica said. "What if he doesn't know what's going on until it's too late? Mom will be gone, and his life will be ruined."

Elizabeth shook her head. "Jessica, I'm not going to listen to you anymore." With that she turned and headed for the den.

Just then, the pizza arrived. Mr. Wakefield

paid the delivery boy and carried the hot carton into the den.

"Clear the decks, gang," he declared. "The food's here."

"Just in time, Dad," Steven said. He grabbed a slice and pointed at the television. "The game's starting."

"Tell Jessica to come down and eat, would you, Elizabeth?" her father asked.

Elizabeth nodded and went into the hallway. "Pizza's here," she called up the stairs. "Want any?"

"I'm not hungry," Jessica yelled back. Elizabeth shrugged and went back into the den.

"She'll be down in a little while," she said, placing a piece of pizza on a plate and cutting it with a fork. "Dad?"

"Umm?"

"How did you and Mom—"

She was interrupted by an explosion of cheering from her brother and father.

"What an unbelievable shot!" Mr. Wakefield exclaimed.

"Way to go!" Steven crowed, waving his fists over his head.

Mr. Wakefield glanced at Elizabeth. "I'm sorry, honey. What did you say?"

"Well, I was just curious," she began again. "How did you and Mom meet?"

He tilted his head up to look at her. "What's this all about, anyway?"

She described the Living History project, and told him how she, Amy, and Pamela had come up with the Sweet Valley Sweethearts idea.

"Was it love at first sight?" she asked.

"Love at what, Elizabeth?" her father murmured absentmindedly. He had obviously not heard a word she'd said.

"At first sight," she repeated loudly. "Did you know Mom was the girl for you the moment you saw her?"

"Hmm . . . Well, I guess so."

There was suddenly a lot of cheering on the television again. "Looks like another championship year," Mr. Wakefield pronounced grandly.

"Number one!" Steven yelled hoarsely, "Number one!"

Elizabeth looked at her brother in disgust. The interview was getting nowhere. She was about to give up when she heard the front door slam and Mrs. Wakefield call out, "Hi, everybody. I'm home."

"Boy, am I glad to see you!" Elizabeth sang out happily, as she ran to meet her.

"Me, too!" Jessica chimed in from the top of the stairs.

"What a day." Mrs. Wakefield sighed loudly as she put her briefcase down on the floor by the front door. She collapsed onto the living room couch and sighed. "I am simply exhausted. And I'm not even done. Elizabeth, will you bring me a glass of water?"

"Sure, Mom." Elizabeth ran toward the kitchen.

"Did you eat yet?" Jessica said. "We sent out for pizza."

"Oh. Thanks, but I already ate. I grabbed a bite on the way home."

"Mom, I'm doing a Living History report for social studies class," Elizabeth said, after she handed the glass of water to her mother.

"That's interesting, dear," her mother replied, flipping through an envelope filled with papers.

"And she chose you and Dad for her subject," Jessica added pointedly.

"Mmm. That's nice."

"So can I interview you now?" Elizabeth finished. "It's kind of important."

Mrs. Wakefield didn't raise her head from her work. "I guess so. Sure."

Elizabeth took a deep breath and dove in. "Did you and Dad fall in love at first sight?"

"How did you meet?" Jessica asked. "Was it incredibly romantic?"

"Or a complete surprise, like a chance encounter in an airport?" Elizabeth added.

"One at a time," Mrs. Wakefield protested, holding up her hands. She sat up as if to answer, but then she said, "I'm sorry, Elizabeth, I am so tired, and it's a long story. Could you ask me again tomorrow?" She heaved herself up and headed for the stairs. "I'll be in better shape to tell you about it then. Good night, girls."

"Mom! Aren't you even going to say good night to Dad?" Jessica cried out after her.

"Oh, I almost forgot he was here," Mrs. Wakefield murmured. "Silly me." She stuck her head into the den and called, "Good night, you two. I'm going right up to bed."

Mr. Wakefield and Steven were still glued to the basketball game. Mr. Wakefield glanced up and blew his wife a kiss.

"Steven, did you do your homework?" Mrs. Wakefield asked. Steven nodded without looking up. "OK, then. See you tomorrow, everybody."

Jessica and Elizabeth watched her leave them with a growing sense of dread.

"Did you hear that? She almost forgot Dad was here," Jessica repeated.

"And she wasn't excited about telling us how they fell in love, either," Elizabeth whispered.

"That's because she's in love with somebody else," Jessica whispered back. "We've got to do something before it's too late!"

"But what?"

"Meet me in my room. I'll get Steven. It's time he knew what's been going on around here."

Elizabeth nodded and hurried up the stairs. Jessica squared her shoulders and marched into the den. "Steven," she announced. "Elizabeth and I have to talk to you, *now!*"

Steven looked up at her, an angry reply on his lips, but the intense look on her face stopped him. He seemed to know immediately that something serious was up. Without another word he followed Jessica out of the room.

"What's all the secrecy for?" Steven asked, once they had gathered in Jessica's room. "Are we planning another surprise party?"

"No!" Jessica hissed. "We're really concerned about Mom."

"What's wrong with Mom?" Steven asked.

Elizabeth took a deep breath and began. "Steven, we think Mom has been spending too much time with a man named Frank Howard."

"Is he the guy she was with yesterday?" Steven asked.

"What do you mean, 'yesterday'?" Jessica pounced on her brother's words.

"Well, I was downtown and I passed the Ritz Cafe and Mom was having lunch with some guy."

"Was he really, really handsome?" Jessica asked.

Steven shrugged. "I guess so."

"What did Mom say to you?" Elizabeth asked.

"Nothing. I waved to her but she was so busy talking, she didn't see me."

Jessica and Elizabeth looked at each other, eyes wide. Jessica's words were barely a whisper. "That proves it."

Elizabeth swallowed hard and nodded at her sister.

"What does it prove?" Steven looked from one twin to the other.

"Steven," Elizabeth said gently, "we think Mom has fallen in love with Mr. Howard."

"That super-handsome, rich man you saw her with yesterday," Jessica added.

"What? You two are nuts!" Steven said in disbelief.

Jessica shook her head. "We are not! We know all about *that* man. He lives in Beverly Hills in this fabulous mansion. It's got a huge pool, tennis courts, and lots and lots of bedrooms!"

"Whoa!" Steven held up one hand. "How do you know all this?"

"Mom showed us an article that was written about him in *Designer's Monthly*. It had a lot of pictures of his mansion," Elizabeth explained.

"Oh, Lizzie!" Jessica suddenly covered her mouth in horror. "Do you think Mom showed us those pictures for a reason?"

"What reason?" Steven was completely confused.

"Maybe she wanted us to see the mansion that we'd be living in."

"Wait a minute," Steven cut in. "She didn't show me the pictures."

Jessica paced around the room. "I wonder what it will be like living in a forty room mansion. I mean, it's practically a castle."

Elizabeth hopped up off the bed. "Jessica, stop talking like that. I don't want to leave Dad."

Jessica spun to face her twin. "Well, I don't either."

"Then don't even think about it."

"You're right. I'd probably hate it in Beverly Hills. I mean, they have so many stars and beautiful people, nobody would notice me."

Steven's voice cracked as he said, "I don't want Mom and Dad to split up. That'd really be awful!"

Elizabeth folded her arms in front of her and put on her most adult voice. "Then we had better take action."

Jessica nodded enthusiastically. "We need a foolproof plan."

Jessica sat on the edge of her bed and bit her lip thoughtfully. "I think we should devise a way to drive Mom and Mr. Howard apart."

"You mean, scare him off?" Steven asked.

"That's it!" Jessica jumped up off the bed. "We'll make Mr. Howard think we're the worst kids on earth."

"Great!" Steven slammed his fist in his hand. "We'll be loud and rude—"

"And insulting," Jessica added. "We'll wear ugly, dirty clothes. Mr. Howard won't know what hit him."

Elizabeth, who hated being mean, hesitated. "I don't know about this. That seems a little too extreme."

"Extreme?" Jessica protested. "We're trying to save our parents' marriage! Now we just have to find a way to see Mr. Howard."

"I say we go with Jessica's plan." Steven held his hand out and Jessica placed hers on top of it.

Elizabeth looked first at her brother and then at her sister and choked back a sob. She realized how much she loved them both and how awful it would be if the family ever split up.

She very solemnly placed her hand on top of theirs. "Count me in."

Five
◇

On Saturday they had a chance to put their plan into action. Mrs. Wakefield had some designs she needed to deliver to Mr. Howard.

"I'll take them, Mom," Jessica said. "I can ride them over on my bike."

Before Mrs. Wakefield had a chance to say no, Jessica had grabbed the designs and raced upstairs to change her clothes and tell Elizabeth.

"This is it, Lizzie," Jessica called. "Operation Shock Mr. Howard."

Five minutes later she tiptoed into her sister's room. Elizabeth was shocked. "You look terrible!"

Jessica had put on an old striped blouse she had outgrown two years before. The sleeves were too short and she had deliberately buttoned it up wrong. She was wearing a pair of plaid shorts that clashed with the blouse.

Jessica smiled. "Thanks. So do you."

Elizabeth was wearing a faded orange sweatshirt with holes in the elbows. She also had on a purple-and-green patchwork skirt that she'd worn in a play at school.

They had both combed gel through their hair to make it look stringy.

"Do you think this stuff will ever wash out?" Elizabeth asked, patting her head with distaste.

"Of course it will," Jessica replied, feeling her own hair gingerly. "It's just styling gel. But it makes us look like we haven't washed our hair in three weeks."

They tiptoed down the stairs and, just as they were leaving, Jessica called, "We're on our way to Mr. Howard's, Mom."

"Do you have his address?" their mother called back. "It's on the right-hand corner of the plans."

"I see it," Elizabeth shouted. "'Bye."

"Hurry back," Mrs. Wakefield said. "I'm going to start lunch soon."

They pedaled fast to reach Mr. Howard's office building. As they turned the corner, Jessica yelled, "There he is. That's him!"

Elizabeth almost fell off her bike when she saw who Jessica was pointing at. "Wow," she whispered. "He really does look like a movie star."

Mr. Howard was standing in front of the building's glass doors, talking to another man. He was even more handsome than Elizabeth could have imagined—tall, tanned, with blue eyes that sparkled.

"Now's our chance," Jessica said, hopping off her bike and propping it up on its kickstand. "Let's go!" Grabbing the folder of designs out of her basket, Jessica dashed toward the man. Elizabeth climbed off her bike, gulped nervously, and hurried after her twin.

"Mr. Howard! Mr. Howard!" Jessica waved and ran straight up to him. He turned at the sound of his name, a pleasant smile on his face. The smile faded to a look of shock when he saw the strangely dressed duo in front of him.

"Hi, Mr. Howard. I'm Jessica Wakefield and this is my sister, Elizabeth."

"You're Alice Wakefield's daughters?" he asked, an uncertain look on his face.

"She asked us to bring these plans to your office," Jessica continued. "I'm glad we caught up with you."

"Thanks," Mr. Howard said, looking them up

and down curiously. "Looks like you two have been doing some yard work today, hmm?"

"Oh, no," Jessica answered. "This is how we always dress. Right, Elizabeth?" Elizabeth nodded.

"Always?" Mr. Howard was staring at their clothes in amazement.

"You see, Mom designs all of our outfits," Jessica explained. "Don't you think she has wonderful taste?" Jessica took a full spin for him.

Mr. Howard looked too shocked to reply.

"I bet she'd love to design a suit for you," Jessica said.

"Oh, that's all right," he replied hastily. "I've got tailors of my own."

"Are you sure?" Jessica persisted.

He nodded quickly.

"Oh, well. It's your loss." She grabbed Elizabeth by the hand and dragged her down the sidewalk. "See you around."

As soon as they were out of sight, the twins fell back against the side of the building, laughing like crazy.

"He must think Mom is the strangest designer who ever lived!" Elizabeth motioned to her twin to peek around the corner back at Mr. Howard.

He hadn't moved. He shook his head slowly, a dazed look on his face. Then he waved goodbye to his friend and went into the building.

As they got on their bikes and headed home, Elizabeth said, "I just hope we don't get into trouble."

"Don't worry," Jessica reassured her sister. "I bet we never see him again!"

An hour later, Jessica and Elizabeth had washed their hair and changed their clothes and were setting the table for lunch when the doorbell rang.

"I'll get it!" Jessica called to her mother in the kitchen. She waltzed to the front window and peeked out through the curtain. When she saw who it was, her knees almost buckled.

"It's Mr. Howard!" she whispered to her sister. "He's here!"

"What should we do?" Elizabeth asked. "I never thought he'd come to the house."

At that moment Steven appeared at the top of the stairs. Jessica, thinking fast, hissed, "Steven, it's *him*. Turn up the stereo and be obnoxious!"

"Sure thing!" Steven grinned and raced into the living room. Then the twins casually opened the front door.

"Well!" Mr. Howard's eyes widened at their

very different appearance. He quickly recovered and flashed them a dazzling smile. "Hello. I barely recognized you two. Is your mother in?"

Jessica cupped one hand over her ear. "You'll have to speak up. I can't hear you!"

Mr. Howard leaned forward and said, more loudly, "Maybe if you turned the music down, it would be a little easier to converse."

"Good idea." Jessica turned and screeched, "Ste-ven! Turn that down!"

The music stopped immediately and Elizabeth smiled at Mr. Howard. "That's our brother, Steven."

"He always plays his music that loud!" Jessica added.

Elizabeth was afraid they were pushing things a little too far so she said cheerfully, "Come on in, Mr. Howard. Mom's in the kitchen."

Mr. Howard relaxed a little at her politeness. "Why, thank you."

Then Steven danced into the room, wearing headphones and moving in jerks and fits.

"It's useless trying to talk to him," Jessica explained. "He hardly ever takes those off."

"Mom, Mr. Howard is here," Elizabeth called toward the kitchen.

"Frank?" Mrs. Wakefield sailed into the room, removing her apron. "What a nice surprise!" The twins watched closely as Mr. Howard and their mother shook hands.

"I initialed the changes you made on the plans," Mr. Howard said. "So I thought I'd just drop them by." He handed Mrs. Wakefield the thick manila envelope and smiled. "I'm very impressed with your work, Alice."

Mrs. Wakefield smiled back and a deep red blush colored her cheeks. "Why, thank you, Frank."

Jessica made a move to usher Mr. Howard back to the front door when Mrs. Wakefield said, "Why don't you join us for lunch? Unfortunately, my husband had to go to the office today, but I was just about to sit down with the kids."

Jessica held her breath, waiting for his answer. Her heart sank as he said, "I'd love to."

The twins exchanged worried looks behind his back.

"You kids go and wash your hands," Mrs. Wakefield instructed, "while I pour Mr. Howard a glass of iced tea."

"Sure, Mom." Jessica and Elizabeth raced to the upstairs bathroom.

Steven appeared in the doorway. "Now that we've got him here, what do we do?"

"It's time for Plan Two!"

"I don't remember a Plan Two," Elizabeth said

as she joined her sister at the bathroom sink. "When did we come up with that?"

"Just now, and it's perfect!" Jessica dried her hands on the towel. "We're going to kill him with kindness! And then we'll spice up his food."

Jessica ran down to the kitchen, followed by Elizabeth. "Mom, why don't you join Mr. Howard in the dining room. Elizabeth and I can handle everything."

When their mother was out of the kitchen, Jessica whispered to Elizabeth, "Wait till he gets a taste of my special salad dressing."

"What?"

Jessica threw open the refrigerator door and began tossing different-size jars and spices onto the counter. "Lizzie, you prepare individual salad plates while I whip up my special spicy dressing."

"Right!" Elizabeth dished large portions of chef salad onto five plates. Then she poured Italian dressing on four of them.

"If this doesn't get him," Jessica giggled as she ladled her special dressing onto Mr. Howard's salad, "I don't know what will."

"What's in it?" Elizabeth asked, setting the plates on a bright yellow tray.

"Molasses, garlic, catsup, soy sauce, and my secret ingredient—hot chili peppers!"

Before Elizabeth could say another word, Jessica swung open the door to the dining room and announced, "Ladies and gentlemen, lunch is served."

Once everyone had their plates, Mrs. Wakefield raised her glass of iced tea. "I would just like to say welcome to our guest. *Bon appétit.*"

Jessica raised her eyebrows at Elizabeth. They both knew that Mrs. Wakefield only used French when she was trying to impress people.

The twins each picked up their salad forks and paused to watch Mr. Howard take his first bite of Jessica's special concoction.

He chewed carefully for a second. Then his eyes widened and he started coughing.

"Frank, are you OK?" Mrs. Wakefield asked, scooting her chair back.

"Water!" he wailed. He was barely able to choke out the word.

"I'll get it!" Jessica leaped to her feet and raced into the kitchen, happy for an excuse to hide her laughter.

Elizabeth bit her lip and stared hard at her plate, trying not to laugh. Steven, knowing his sisters must have done something to Mr. Howard's salad, was smiling.

Jessica returned with a tall glass of water which she handed to Mr. Howard. Tears were streaming down his cheeks. "Thank you," he said gratefully. "I think the salad dressing went down the wrong way."

"That dressing is Mom's specialty," Jessica said, with a twinkle in her eye. "We have it practically every day. Isn't it good?"

Mr. Howard took a long sip of water and then nodded. "It certainly is different. So, uh . . . spicy and different."

"Spicy?" Mrs. Wakefield looked at Jessica in confusion.

Before Mr. Howard could say another word, Jessica reached for his plate. "I'm glad you like it, Mr. Howard. I'll bring you some more."

"No!" Mr. Howard nearly knocked over his chair trying to stand up. "No, thank you. I'm really pretty full. I had a big breakfast."

"Oh." Jessica set the salad back in front of him. "Well, I hope you have room for Mom's special casserole. It really goes well with the salad."

Mrs. Wakefield blushed. "Jessica, you certainly are full of compliments today."

Jessica smiled her sweetest smile at her mother. "I just want Mr. Howard to know what a good cook you are."

"I-I'm sure she is," Mr. Howard said, placing his napkin on the table. "Unfortunately, I'm afraid I can't stay for the rest of this, uh, delicious lunch.

Please forgive me, but I just remembered a special meeting that was scheduled for this afternoon."

Mrs. Wakefield looked completely bewildered. "I'm sorry you have to leave so soon, Frank. Maybe we can have lunch another time."

Mr. Howard nodded vigorously. "Let's plan on it."

Mrs. Wakefield started to stand up, but he stopped her. "No, Alice, please don't get up. I know my way out."

"We'll walk you to the door," Jessica announced. She grabbed her sister's hand. "Come on, Elizabeth."

"I hope you do come back, Mr. Howard," Jessica said. "Mom is famous for her unusual dishes."

Mr. Howard tried to smile. "I'll bet she is."

Jessica's voice squeaked as she said, "It's too bad you didn't get a chance to meet the rest of our brothers and sisters."

"The rest?" Mr. Howard looked very confused. "I thought there was only three of you."

"Living in Sweet Valley," Jessica explained quickly. "But we've got lots of half-sisters and -brothers around California. They're from Mom's first two marriages." Jessica lowered her voice and added, "We're hoping this one will last."

"Well, I think your mother is a wonderful designer and a fine woman," Mr. Howard said, stepping out the front door. "She really seems to have come a long way."

He backed away slowly, almost tripping over the stone planter at the end of the walk. As he was getting into his car Jessica called out, "Be sure and come back soon. We'll have Mom make her special tuna casserole. It's really unusual."

The last the twins saw of Mr. Howard was his startled face disappearing into the car. The sight made them burst out laughing. "Jess, you're terrible!" Elizabeth managed to say.

"I know," Jessica whispered between giggles. "But remember, it's for the family."

As they watched him speed off down the road, Elizabeth wondered out loud, "Do you think that'll stop him from liking Mom?"

Jessica's tears of laughter suddenly stopped. "Oh, Lizzie, I hope so," she said softly. "I really do!"

Six
◇

Elizabeth met Amy at the park on Monday afternoon. The two of them walked over to Pamela's house where they were supposed to do more work on their Living History project. Lately, though, Elizabeth hadn't been able to concentrate on anything. Her stomach was always in a knot from worrying about her parents. Neither of them had ever gotten around to telling her how they first met. And that made her worry even more.

"Elizabeth," Amy asked, after they had walked an entire block in silence. "Is something wrong?"

"No!" Elizabeth replied, a little too quickly. "Why?"

"Well, for the last few days you've been so

quiet. I thought you might be sick or something."

Elizabeth shook her head miserably. "I'm not sick."

"Well, are you mad at me?" Amy stared down at her feet.

"Of course not, Amy!" Elizabeth couldn't hold her secret in any longer. Before she knew it, the entire story had tumbled out of her mouth, starting with the forgotten anniversary and ending with the lunch with Mr. Howard.

"I'm really afraid my parents are going to break up." Elizabeth fought hard to hold back her tears.

Amy patted Elizabeth's shoulder. "You know, a lot of parents get busy with their work, but that doesn't mean they don't love each other. Are you sure you're not imagining things?"

"But it's not just me," Elizabeth protested. "Jessica feels the same way."

"Well, you know what a wild imagination Jessica has. She always exaggerates."

That was true. With Jessica things were either really awful or really wonderful. There was never any in-between.

Elizabeth tucked a strand of hair behind one ear. "I guess you're right. It's just that my parents have been apart so much lately—"

"But you said your father was all tied up, working on that important case."

"I know—"

"And your mother has a big new account."

Elizabeth nodded. "With a *really* handsome, *really* rich man."

"So?" Amy shrugged. "I think your father is really handsome."

Elizabeth smiled gratefully at her friend.

"Look," Amy said, "my parents are always working late. They end up leaving messages for each other on the refrigerator door."

Elizabeth couldn't help laughing at that. "Really?"

Amy put her hand on her chest. "Cross my heart."

Elizabeth suddenly felt relieved. She was lucky to have such a good friend. As they strolled along, she thought, *Amy's right. Lots of families get busy and don't fall apart. Why should mine?*

At the Jacobsons' house, Amy reached up to ring the doorbell, but before her finger touched the buzzer, the door flew open. Pamela stood just inside, a big grin on her face.

"Hi! Come on in! I've got a surprise for you."

Mrs. Jacobson was standing in the living room behind Pamela. "Hello, girls," she said, "I'm taking everyone to Casey's Place for a Sooper-Dooper Banana Scooper."

Elizabeth pointed to her notebook. "But what about the project?"

"I've finished my interview with my parents and so has Amy," Pamela said. "I've completed my report on romantic couples in literature, like Romeo and Juliet. And Amy collected love sonnets by Shakespeare."

Elizabeth stared down at the notebook she was holding. She had made a list of a few romantic couples in history, but she hadn't even begun her library research. Elizabeth's cheeks burned. She was holding up the entire project.

Amy noticed her blush and said quickly, "We've still got a whole week till the report is due. That's lots of time. We should take an ice cream break."

Elizabeth smiled shyly at Mrs. Jacobson. "Well, OK. Let's go! It's too hard to turn down a Casey's Special."

At Casey's Place, the most popular ice cream parlor in Sweet Valley, Mrs. Jacobson ordered four banana splits at the counter.

"Let's sit over here!" Pamela skipped over to the round table by the window. Elizabeth smiled. She knew why Pamela wanted to sit by the window. A lot of the kids from Sweet Valley Middle

School came to the mall and this was the perfect place to watch them go by.

"Oh, look, there's Bruce Patman." Pamela pointed to the dark-haired boy leaning against one of the pillars by the escalators. Bruce was one of the cutest, and most conceited, boys in the seventh grade.

"And Jerry McAllister and Charlie Cashman are with him," Elizabeth said, dipping her spoon into her banana split.

"So what else is new?" Amy cracked. "Those boys stick together like glue." All three girls giggled as they dug into their ice cream.

Suddenly, her mouth full, Amy said, "Hey, Elizabeth! Isn't that your mom?"

Amy pointed toward a woman looking at the display window of Brass and Glass, a fancy furniture store at the mall. Her mother's back was turned but Elizabeth recognized her immediately. She also recognized the man standing next to her.

"Oh, no," Elizabeth cried. Their plan to scare Mr. Howard away had obviously not worked at all. Her mother was still seeing him and she looked happier than ever.

"Is anything wrong, Elizabeth?" Mrs. Jacobson asked.

"No!" Elizabeth fumbled for her napkin and

pretended to wipe her lap. "I spilled some ice cream on myself. That's all."

As Elizabeth dabbed at her skirt, she raised her eyes to meet Amy's. Amy mouthed the words, "Is that him?"

Elizabeth nodded.

"Are those your parents?" Mrs. Jacobson asked, as Mr. Howard and Mrs. Wakefield stepped into the store.

"That's my mother and a client of hers." Elizabeth tried to sound as calm as possible. "My mom's a decorator. She often takes her clients shopping."

"That's strange," Mrs. Jacobson said, staring at the store across from them.

"What is?" Pamela asked, following her mother's gaze.

"This may sound silly, but I think someone is following them." Mrs. Jacobson pointed with her spoon toward a pillar. "Look."

A figure in a long trench coat and large felt hat peeked out from behind the marble pillar, then scurried in little steps to the door of Brass and Glass. From the pocket of the tan coat, the person took out a newspaper and pretended to read.

Elizabeth nearly choked on her banana split. She recognized the coat and hat as her mother's, but the tennis shoes definitely belonged to her sister!

"Jessica!"

"Where?" Pamela looked back to where Bruce and the boys were still gathered. "Is she here, too?"

Elizabeth was relieved to find no one had recognized her sister as the person in the trench coat.

"Wh-what I mean is," Elizabeth stammered, "Jessica and I were supposed to meet here. I almost forgot. She's probably waiting for me in front of Sweet Valley Fashions right now."

Elizabeth sprang to her feet and thanked Mrs. Jacobson for the ice cream. "I'll talk to you guys later," she said to Pamela and Amy.

"Call me tonight!" Amy called out after her.

Elizabeth nodded and raced out of the restaurant.

She had to figure out how to communicate with Jessica without letting Amy, Pamela, and Mrs. Jacobson see her. She marched straight to the door of the furniture store and pretended to wave at her mother. At the same time she whispered out of the corner of her mouth, "Count to thirty, then follow me." Then she added, "And Jessica, we're being watched, so act natural!"

As soon as they were safely out of view, Elizabeth put her hands on her hips and shook her head at her sister. "What do you think you're doing?"

"I'm following Mom." Jessica took off her hat and shook out her long blond hair. "We were at home having a snack when the phone rang. It was Mr. Howard calling to tell Mom to meet him at the mall. I thought I'd better follow them so I hopped on a bus and came down here."

"Well, did you find out anything?"

Jessica nodded sadly. "Oh, Lizzie, it doesn't look good. They've been shopping for china and silverware together."

Elizabeth took a deep breath to calm herself. "Remember, Mom is a decorator. She's always running off with clients to shop for furniture and stuff."

A familiar laugh interrupted their conversation. Both girls held their breath as their mother and Mr. Howard passed right by them. Jessica peeked out from their alcove to watch them.

"What are they doing now?" Elizabeth asked.

"They're going into Sweet Valley Jewelry Store," Jessica answered.

"What are they going in *there* for?"

Jessica's voice was barely a whisper. "Oh, Lizzie, they're looking at engagement rings!"

"Jess, no!" Elizabeth covered her mouth in horror.

Jessica nodded and her voice shook. "How many decorators do you know who choose their client's engagement rings?"

Seven
◇

Dear Elizabeth,

I've got a plan. Meet me in front
of Dad's office at 3:30. I'll be
waiting.

Love, Jess

Jessica read the note she had written and her eyes
started to fill with tears. Seeing their mother looking at rings with Mr. Howard had been very
upsetting. Once their mother had left, she and
Elizabeth had gone into Sweet Valley Jewelry
Store to see the ring for themselves. It was
beautiful—a huge diamond surrounded by tiny
sapphires. This just *had* to be a bad dream, and
Jessica was going to end it once and for all.

Jessica folded the note, tucked it into Elizabeth's locker, and turned to run to her next class. She was in such a hurry that she almost crashed into Janet Howell, one of the most popular girls in the eighth grade and president of the Unicorn Club.

"Hi, Jessica. Don't forget about the big meeting this afternoon."

"Meeting?" Jessica's mind was a blur.

"Of course," Janet said. "Today's the day we talk about the service award. You remember, don't you? The one that's to be awarded to the organization that does the most good in the community." She smiled knowingly. "I'm sure you'll have some great ideas."

"Is that today?" Jessica fell back against one of the lockers. Ever since Mr. Howard had come on the scene, she'd forgotten everything else.

"Of course it's today!" Janet exclaimed. "And *all* members should be there."

For a half-second Jessica debated whether to run back and remove the note from Elizabeth's locker, or to go ahead with her plan. Then the bell rang, and she knew she wouldn't have time to retrieve the note.

"I'm sorry, Janet," Jessica said. "But I can't be there today."

The older girl raised her eyebrows in disapproval, but before she could say anything else, Jessica broke away and ran down the hall. "'Bye, Janet," she called over her shoulder.

For a moment Jessica felt awful. Janet Howell would think she didn't care about being a Unicorn. But that didn't really matter now.

I've got more important things to worry about, she thought. *Like saving Mom and Dad's marriage.*

"So what's your plan?" Elizabeth asked, as she joined Jessica on the sidewalk. They were standing in front of the plate glass doors leading into the offices of Mr. Wakefield's law firm.

"Elizabeth," her twin declared, "it's time to tell Dad what's going on between Mom and Mr. Howard."

"Do you really think that's a good idea, Jess? Isn't there anything else we can do?"

"Like what?" Jessica shot back. "We can't stand by and just let Mr. Howard take Mom away from us."

"But what will Dad do?"

"I don't know." Jessica pursed her lips in thought. "I hope he doesn't try to shoot Mr. Howard or anything."

"Daddy would never hurt anybody," Elizabeth said quickly.

"Well, he *is* a lawyer. Maybe he'll just sue Mr. Howard for millions and millions of dollars." A small smile crept across Jessica's face. "You know, that wouldn't be such a bad idea."

"How are we going to tell him?" Elizabeth asked.

"Elizabeth," Jessica said sternly. "We can't be cowards about this. We have to stick together and tell Dad so he can bring Mom to her senses. Then things can be just the way they used to be."

Elizabeth wiped her nose with a tissue and nodded. "You're right. Let's go."

Within minutes they were ushered into their father's office by his secretary. He looked up from his desk in surprise. "Well, to what do I owe this delightful interruption?"

Jessica opened her mouth to speak, then shut it. Her father sat in front of them, grinning widely. He seemed so pleased to see them, she didn't have the heart to tell him her bad news.

"How's your big case going, Dad?" she finally blurted out.

"I'm very glad you asked." He folded his hands in front of him. "It should be all wrapped up by tomorrow and . . ." He paused dramatically. "It looks like we're going to win!"

"Oh, Dad, that's great!" Elizabeth rushed forward and wrapped her arms around his neck. She fought hard to hold back her tears. Just thinking about her mother leaving her wonderful father made her want to cry.

"That's terrific, Dad." Jessica ran to hug him, too.

"Hey, what's all this?" he asked, looking pleased at his daughters' attention.

"We just want you to know we love you and—" Elizabeth's eyes misted up again and she couldn't go on. "And we've missed you lately," Jessica finished for her. "An awful lot."

"Well, I've missed you, too," Mr. Wakefield replied. "Which is why I'm going to take us all out to a big dinner tomorrow night to celebrate."

Jessica and Elizabeth exchanged quick looks over their father's head. Being a twin was a big advantage at times like this because they each knew what the other was thinking.

"Dad, I've got an idea," Jessica said. "Why don't you take Mom out instead?"

Elizabeth nodded eagerly. "To a special restaurant."

"Then you could have a romantic dinner for two by candlelight," Jessica added. She was sure it was their only hope.

"Oh, and find one with a violin player that

comes to your table and serenades you," Elizabeth said dreamily.

Mr. Wakefield chuckled. "Listen to you two. You sound like a pair of matchmakers."

"Well, you forgot your own anniversary," Jessica reminded him, putting her hands on her hips. "I think you owe it to Mom to treat her to a special dinner."

"I do, too," Elizabeth said.

Mr. Wakefield looked from one daughter to the other. "Is this an order?" he asked.

"Yes!" they said in unison.

"OK, then." He put his arms behind his head and relaxed back in his chair. "You know, that's not a bad idea," he said thoughtfully. "There was this little Italian restaurant over on Seaview Drive that your mother and I used to go to a lot, before we were married. Haven't been back in years."

"Oh, Dad!" Jessica hugged him again. "You have to go there. You just *have* to!"

"OK, OK!" He held his hands up in front of him. "Listen, you two, I've still got work to do this afternoon. If I'm going to win this case, you'd better scoot."

"Yes, sir!" They saluted as they marched out the door.

*   *   *

That night, before she went to bed, Elizabeth tiptoed to Jessica's room and knocked softly on the door.

"Come in."

Jessica was already under the covers. The lamp on the nightstand glowed in the darkened room. "Jess, do you think the dinner will make everything OK between Mom and Dad?" Elizabeth whispered.

"I'm not sure, Lizzie. It's a good start, but just to be on the safe side . . ." Her voice trailed off.

"Jessica, you have that funny look in your eyes."

"What look?" Jessica blinked innocently.

"The one you get when you're planning to do something that will get us into lots of trouble."

"Elizabeth!" Jessica looked offended. "I am not going to get anyone in trouble."

"Promise?"

Jessica drew her face into a pout. "I can't believe you don't believe me."

"Promise?" Elizabeth insisted stubbornly.

Jessica looked at her sister for a moment, then flicked off her bedside lamp.

"Trust me." Jessica's voice came out of the darkness. "Good night, Elizabeth."

Eight

◇

After school on Friday, Jessica hopped on her bike and pedaled straight downtown to Mr. Howard's office. *I'm going to go right up to Mr. Howard and tell him to leave Mom alone.*

She hadn't told Elizabeth about her plan because she knew her sister would have tried to talk her out of it.

"I'll tell him that our family was perfectly fine until he came to Sweet Valley," she said out loud as she rode along. "I'll tell him that Mom and Dad love each other, and if Mom leaves, we'll be orphans. Then I'll politely ask him to go back to Beverly Hills—*alone*."

Jessica swallowed hard. The gleaming steel-

and-glass exterior of Mr. Howard's new office
building loomed in front of her. She locked her
bike in the stand at the entrance and marched to
the elevators, where she headed directly for the
penthouse floor.

The elevator stopped and opened to show a
large reception area. A pleasant-looking woman
with white hair and glasses greeted her. "May I
help you?"

"I'm Jessica Wakefield," Jessica announced,
"and I would like to talk to Mr. Frank Howard,
please."

"Oh, Alice Wakefield's daughter?" the recep-
tionist asked. Jessica nodded and the woman
smiled. "Have a seat, Jessica. I'll tell Mr. Howard
you're here." The woman gestured toward a gray
leather couch set against the wall.

Looking around, Jessica realized that her
mother had done a wonderful job decorating the
office. The thick carpet was a deep shade of ma-
roon. Chrome-and-glass tables holding beautiful
lamps were placed at both ends of the couch. The
wall hangings made the whole room look rich and
elegant.

Just as she was starting to change her mind
about being there, Mr. Howard stepped out from
his office. "Why, Jessica, what a nice surprise!" He

flashed a dazzling smile and once again Jessica noticed how handsome he was.

"Hello, Mr. Howard," Jessica said in her most businesslike voice. She didn't want him to charm her out of her speech. "I was wondering if I could talk to you."

"Certainly." He gestured for her to follow him but the secretary interrupted. "Excuse me, Mr. Howard, but there's a call for you on line one."

"Pardon me, Jessica," he said, moving back to his office. "I'll only be a minute."

She watched him pick up the phone on his desk and then, with one hand, give the door a push. The heavy oak door didn't close all the way.

Jessica had no intention of eavesdropping but his words carried clearly to the reception area. They made her stomach fill with butterflies.

"Darling, how are you?" Mr. Howard said. "I've missed you."

Jessica pursed her lips. *This is worse than I thought. They just saw each other Monday night and they already miss each other.*

"I've got the ring, dear," he went on. "I can't wait until Saturday night. Then we'll be together, once and for all."

"Saturday night!" Jessica sprang up and ran for the elevator. "That's tomorrow!"

"Wait a minute, Jessica," the secretary called after her. "Don't you want to talk to Mr. Howard?"

"It's too late to talk," Jessica said as she flew into the elevator.

Nine

◇

Elizabeth stared down at the blank page in her notebook. It was the final meeting of her Living History group, and once again she wasn't prepared. The three girls were just settling down in the den of the Suttons' house.

"I'll go get us some sodas," Amy announced, jumping up and disappearing into the kitchen.

Pamela got up to call her mother and Elizabeth ran into the kitchen to talk to Amy.

"Amy," Elizabeth whispered. "I don't have my interview."

"Weren't you able to talk to your parents?"

Elizabeth shook her head miserably. "Too many things are going on at home." She looked her best friend in the eye. "I think I'm going to have to drop out of this project."

"Elizabeth, you can't!"

"It's not fair to you and Pamela. If I don't get this done, Mrs. Arnette will give all of us a bad grade."

"Don't worry, Elizabeth. You still have the whole weekend to do it."

"But, Amy, I don't know when I'll be able to talk to my parents." She picked up a glass of soda and followed her friend back into the den.

When they were all seated again, Elizabeth closed her notebook and said, "I'm going to quit. It's better this way, you'll see."

"You can't quit!" Pamela exclaimed. "No matter what's going on with your family, we're all in this together."

Elizabeth looked over at Amy in surprise. "Pamela knows, Elizabeth," Amy explained. "I had to tell her."

Before Elizabeth could respond the doorbell rang and within seconds Jessica burst into the room. She looked as if she had seen a ghost.

She hurriedly recounted the conversation she'd overheard at Mr. Howard's office. Then she sobbed, "Oh, Lizzie, I never believed Mom would go away so soon."

"We've got to stop her!" Elizabeth said with determination.

"We'll help!" Amy and Pamela chimed in.

For the next ten minutes no one said a word. Jessica paced anxiously in the corner. Amy chewed thoughtfully on a piece of apple. Elizabeth concentrated all her energy on thinking up a plan to stop Mr. Howard.

"I've got an idea," Jessica suddenly announced. "It's a long shot, but it just might work!"

"What is it?" Elizabeth demanded, as all three girls leaped to their feet.

"First we need to get Steven out of basketball practice," Jessica said. "Then I'll tell you everything."

The girls hopped off the bus in front of Sweet Valley High, and Jessica led her sister, Pamela, and Amy up the sidewalk to the entrance of the high school gymnasium.

"Good," Jessica said. "The team's still practicing."

They stepped through the doors and were met with the noisy sound of basketballs pounding against the wooden floor, mingled with shouts and the squeak of sneakers. Steven, who played on the junior varsity team, was one of the players on the court.

"I hope we can get him away to talk," Elizabeth said to Amy, a worried frown on her face. "We don't have much time."

Just then the coach blew his whistle and all the boys jogged toward the sidelines.

"Good workout, guys," the coach said. "Hit the showers." As they obediently filed by, he tossed a fresh towel at each one. "See you tomorrow."

Steven was just about to disappear into the locker room when Jessica caught his attention.

"Steven Wakefield!" she called out loudly. "Get over here!"

Steven turned around and jogged toward them, a huge grin on his face. "So you came to see the star in action, did you?"

Elizabeth could tell that Jessica was going to snap back at him and quickly said, "Steven, we need your help. It's really important."

He looked closely from one twin to the other, then nodded. "What is it?"

"Mom is going to elope with Mr. Howard tomorrow night," Jessica exclaimed.

"What!" Steven looked aghast at the news.

"That's right," Elizabeth chimed in. "Jessica

heard him planning it with her on the phone at his office."

"It's true, Steven," Jessica said solemnly. "We have to do something fast to stop them."

"But what can we do?" he sputtered.

Jessica crossed her arms. "We're going to convince Mr. Howard, once and for all, that getting involved with our mother would be the worst disaster in the world."

"How are we going to do that?"

"Mr. Howard is coming to our house for dinner tonight—that is, after I invite him."

"But Mom and Dad are going out."

"That's right!" Jessica's eyes gleamed. "After they leave, Mr. Howard will arrive and meet the *real* Wakefield children—all *ten* of them."

"Ten?" Steven cocked his head in confusion.

"That's right. From all of Mom's marriages."

"Oh." Steven chuckled. "I get it."

Jessica smiled with satisfaction. "He'll wish he'd never heard of any of the Wakefields after tonight."

"We're going to need lots of people to help," Elizabeth said hurriedly.

Steven turned and raced for the locker room. "Meet me outside in five minutes," he shouted over his shoulder.

The four girls hurried outside the gym and anxiously paced back and forth in front of the exit. True to his word, Steven emerged from the locker room minutes later. Behind him trooped six lanky members of the basketball team.

"Will these volunteers do?" he asked, a huge grin on his face.

"Oh, Steven, they're perfect!" Elizabeth said, grinning widely.

"Come on, everyone," Jessica ordered happily, clapping her hands. "Follow me. I'll explain what you have to do on the way home."

"Jessica!" Elizabeth grabbed her sister by the sleeve and pulled her to a stop. "We haven't called and invited Mr. Howard yet. What if he's made other plans?"

"Oh, that's right." Jessica slapped her forehead. "We'd better find a phone."

"There's one by the grocery two blocks from school," one of the basketball players said.

They ran down the street. Jessica stepped into the phone booth and pulled the door shut. Elizabeth watched anxiously as her sister dialed the number. After a brief conversation, Jessica hung up the phone, stepped out of the booth, and smiled slyly. "I talked to his secretary. She actually believed I was Mom. Mr. Howard is coming over at seven-fifteen."

"Seven-fifteen?" Elizabeth repeated. "But Mom and Dad aren't leaving for dinner until seven o'clock. What if they're late and they run into Mr. Howard?"

"We'll just have to make sure they leave on time, that's all."

"What's the plan, Jessica?" Steven asked impatiently.

"OK, everybody, listen carefully." Jessica raised her voice a little so the whole group could hear. "I want you all to go home and put on the oldest, dirtiest clothes you have. Then I want you to come over to our house at exactly five after seven."

"What'll we do when we get there?" the tallest basketball player asked.

Jessica smiled and answered sweetly. "You'll see."

Ten

◇

At two minutes to seven, Mrs. Wakefield was still upstairs, putting on her earrings. Mr. Wakefield stood waiting for her in front of the television, catching the end of the sports report.

"Mom!" Jessica called up the stairs. She was almost frantic. "You're going to be late!"

"Don't worry, Jessica," her father called. "This restaurant is pretty casual. They'll hold a table for us."

"When was the last time you were there?" Jessica demanded.

Mr. Wakefield scratched his head. "Gosh, I don't know. Years ago?"

"Well, things could have changed," Jessica practically shrieked. Her father looked up in surprise.

"She's right, Dad," Steven joined in. "If De-Salvio's takes reservations, they probably want you to stick to them. In fact, I hear it's become one of the hot spots in town."

"Really? Maybe you're right." Mr. Wakefield turned off the television set. "I'd better hurry your mother along."

"She's on her way," Elizabeth announced from upstairs. She was guiding her mother down the hall toward the stairs.

"Wait a minute, Elizabeth," her mother protested, trying to turn around. "I don't have my purse."

Elizabeth waved her bag in the air. "It's right here. Your lipstick and brush are inside."

"Boy, the way you kids are scurrying around tonight," Mrs. Wakefield said with a smile, "you'd think you were trying to get rid of us." She tucked the bag under her arm.

"That's because we've got a wild party planned right after you leave," Steven joked.

Jessica shot him an angry look. "That's not funny, Steven," she snapped.

"He's just kidding, Jess," Elizabeth said hurriedly. "We all want you both to have a terrific time."

"Mom, you look beautiful!" Jessica called from the foot of the stairs. "Doesn't she, Daddy?"

Mr. Wakefield smiled approvingly at his wife.

"She certainly does. Just like the girl I first dated."

Mrs. Wakefield giggled as she came down the steps. "Oh, Ned, don't be silly."

When Mrs. Wakefield reached the bottom of the stairs, Mr. Wakefield kissed her lightly on the cheek. Jessica grabbed her sister's hand and squeezed it with all her strength. "It's working," she whispered.

Elizabeth nodded excitedly.

Steven checked his watch and announced loudly, "It's seven o'clock!"

"You don't want to miss your reservations!" Jessica grabbed her parents' elbows and ushered them out the door. Steven raced down the sidewalk to the car. "Curfew is midnight!" he cracked, holding the door for his mother.

"'Bye! Have a wonderful time," Elizabeth called out. She and Jessica waved gaily as Mr. and Mrs. Wakefield drove off.

As soon as the car rounded the corner, Jessica declared, "Time to get to work."

Elizabeth looked up and down the empty street. There wasn't a sign of the volunteers. "Where is everyone?" she wondered out loud. "Do you think they deserted us?"

There was a violent stirring in the bushes beside the house. The twins turned to see the most outlandish spectacle emerge from behind them.

Amy Sutton led the pack, dressed in a tattered pair of overalls. Mud was streaked over her face and she had arranged her hair into a messy pile on her head.

Pamela Jacobson was right behind her, followed by the boys from Steven's team. They had all gotten into the spirit, wearing baggy, worn jeans and T-shirts smeared with axle grease. No one looked as if he or she had taken a shower in weeks.

Jessica quickly set the group to work. "We've got to pull all the nice furniture from the living room out on the back porch. We can throw a dirty cover over the couch."

"Then we'll bring up the old tattered stuff from the basement," Elizabeth said. "The house will look like a tornado hit it."

They set to work and within minutes the house was a wreck. Elizabeth and Jessica took a second to make sure their own outfits were suitably awful. They had on Steven's old workout clothes which were way too big. Jessica looked her sister over critically, then reached out and enlarged the small hole in her sweatshirt.

"Jessica! What are you doing?"

"Come on, Elizabeth," Jessica chided. "This is no time to get prissy."

Just then the doorbell rang.

"It's him!" Steven whispered from the hall.

"OK, everybody hide!" As the gang ducked out of sight, Elizabeth and Jessica walked to the front door and threw it open.

Mr. Howard was standing on the step, elegantly dressed in a crisp pinstripe suit, a small rose tucked in his lapel. He took a look at the twins and almost lost his balance.

"Why, Mr. Howard," Jessica said, "what a surprise!"

"Please come in." Elizabeth took him by the elbow and ushered him into the hall.

"Surprise?" The man looked confused. "I thought your mother called my secretary and invited me to dinner tonight."

"Oh, you mustn't fall for everything Mom does, you know," Jessica said lightly. "Sometimes, she gets . . . well, a little confused."

"She does?" Mr. Howard looked nervously back toward the front door. Steven shut it firmly behind them.

"Oh, yes," Jessica rattled on. "Sometimes she'll call us down to dinner, when there isn't even any food ready."

"I don't understand."

"Oh, yes," Elizabeth chimed in. She lowered her voice and added, "We're a little worried about

Mother. Lately she's taken to talking to herself again."

"Again?" Mr. Howard blinked his eyes. "Why would she do that?"

The twins looked at him solemnly and mimed someone drinking from a bottle. Jessica added a little hiccup for extra effect.

Elizabeth led him into the ramshackle living room. "Just make yourself comfortable."

Mr. Howard's eyes widened as he surveyed the soiled chair Elizabeth pointed him toward. He positioned himself gingerly on the edge and tried to look comfortable.

"But where's your father?" he asked.

Just then a huge crash came from the hall. The entire gang of basketball players burst into the room, dragging Amy by the arms and legs.

"Wh-what are you doing to that child?" Mr. Howard demanded, leaping to his feet. The two tallest guys looked down at him dumbly, then dropped Amy onto the carpet.

"Nuthin'!" one of them said. "We was jus' horsin' around, like usual."

"Yeah," the other boy said. "We're playin' our favorite game."

"Drop The Sister," another one explained. He made a move to grab Jessica.

"Sister!" Mr. Howard said. "Now, wait a minute. Are all of these children your brothers and sisters?"

"As far as we know," Steven replied. "Of course, it's hard to tell."

"Let's climb up on the roof," one of the boys said as he grabbed Amy again, "and play up there."

"Just a minute!" Mr. Howard ordered. "Hold it right there. You put her down this instant." The boy did as he was told. Then Mr. Howard looked over at Amy and said, "Are you all right?"

She nodded, then grinned at him. It looked as if her front teeth were missing. Elizabeth noticed the shocked look on Mr. Howard's face and tried not to giggle. Steven, however, could not hold back anymore. He burst out laughing and Jessica tried to nudge him back to silence. But the damage was done. The rest of the team began to chuckle, and soon Elizabeth, Amy, and Pamela were laughing, too.

Mr. Howard watched without a word. Finally, when everyone had calmed down a little, he said, "I see what's going on. This is some kind of practical joke." He turned around and glared at Jessica and Elizabeth. "And I am not amused."

Elizabeth watched Mr. Howard march to the front door and she suddenly felt a little ashamed.

"Maybe we've gone too far," she whispered to Jessica.

Her sister shook her head vehemently. "This is exactly what we wanted," she hissed. "Now he'll go back to Los Angeles and leave Mom alone."

Mr. Howard swung open the front door and stopped in his tracks. Elizabeth looked up and nearly fainted with shock. There, framed in the doorway, were Mr. and Mrs. Wakefield.

"Frank? What are you doing here?" Mrs. Wakefield exclaimed.

"*What* has happened to this house?" Mr. Wakefield demanded, gaping at the wreck of a living room. "And who are all of these people?"

"I'm completely confused," Mr. Howard said. "First I receive a call telling me I'm invited to dinner. I cancel a previous engagement to come here. Then, when I arrive, I find out it's all some kind of silly prank."

The room, which had been packed with people, suddenly emptied as Steven's basketball team, Amy, and Pamela hurried out the back door. The Wakefield children were left standing in the middle of the living room, alone.

"I'm sure there must be a good explanation for all of this," Mrs. Wakefield stammered to Mr. Howard.

"There had better be." Mr. Wakefield narrowed his eyes at his children. "I want to hear some talking. And I want to hear it now!"

"Excuse me," a soft voice interrupted. "Is this the Wakefield home?"

Everyone spun around to see a beautiful, dark-haired woman standing in the doorway. She smiled shyly. "I'm looking for Mr. Frank Howard. His secretary told me I might find him here."

"Karen? Is—is that you?" Mr. Howard asked as the beautiful woman peered into the room over Mr. and Mrs. Wakefield's shoulders. "I wasn't expecting you until tomorrow."

Jessica and Elizabeth stared at each other in horror. Mr. Howard was supposed to meet her tomorrow?

Mr. Howard quickly introduced Karen Barclay to the Wakefields as his fiancée.

Out of the corner of her mouth Jessica whispered, "I guess I made a mistake."

Elizabeth slowly turned to face her sister. "You *guess*?"

Steven muttered behind them, "Boy, are we in trouble now!"

Eleven

◇

For the next half hour, the Wakefield children tried to explain their antics to their parents and Mr. Howard. Jessica had to do most of the talking.

She could feel her cheeks getting redder by the minute. Only hours before, there had been no question in her mind that a terrible crisis had hit the family. With each word, however, the whole thing sounded more and more ridiculous.

Mr. Howard and his fiancée Karen sat side by side on the old sofa, holding hands. With each description of how Jessica had discovered a new "clue," his face relaxed more and more. Soon he was grinning. When she told how she had followed them to the jewelry store, Mr. Howard threw back his head and laughed uproariously. Even Mr. and Mrs. Wakefield were smiling.

Finally Jessica shrugged and stared down at her hands. "So, you see, we thought Mr. Howard and Mom were going to elope, tomorrow night."

"And we had to stop it," Steven added. "For your sake, Dad," Elizabeth said. "And for the whole family."

"I can't say that I approve of your methods," Mr. Howard interrupted with a chuckle. "But I admire your determination. Not too many children would go to such lengths to keep their family together."

"Not too many children have the wild imagination our Jessica has," Mr. Wakefield commented, raising an eyebrow at his daughter.

"I don't think it's wild," Jessica protested. "What would you think if your parents forgot their anniversary?"

"We told you, honey," Mrs. Wakefield replied. "We've both been working very hard."

"But you didn't even give each other a present, or flowers, or go out to din—" Jessica stopped in midsentence. "Hey, what are you two doing home, anyway?" she demanded. "This was supposed to be your romantic night out."

Their parents glanced at each other, then Mrs. Wakefield said, "Well, your father and I got to the restaurant and suddenly realized we were missing something."

"What?" the twins and Steven asked.

Their mother smiled at them. "You."

"We wanted to celebrate our wedding anniversary," Mr. Wakefield explained, "but the best part of our marriage has been having you children."

"So we decided to come back and get you," Mrs. Wakefield added. "Of course, we didn't expect to find this." She gestured to the shambles of a living room.

Jessica winced at the reminder. "We'll clean it all up, I promise." Elizabeth and Steven nodded in agreement.

"I know you will," their father said with a smile. "Tonight your mom and I realize we haven't been spending enough time at home. Sometimes it takes a little crisis to remind us all of—"

"Ahem." Mr. Howard cleared his throat. "This sounds like private family talk. I think Karen and I should leave you alone now." The couple stood up to leave.

"No, no," Mrs. Wakefield said, motioning for them to sit back down. "Frank, this concerns you, too." She leaned against the arm of the wingback chair their father sat in. "You see, kids, Mr. Howard has made me a very generous offer. He wants me to redecorate his main offices in Los Angeles."

"Are you going to?" Elizabeth asked, holding her breath.

"I've decided to say no." She smiled at Mr. Howard. "You see, I started decorating as a part-time profession. Lately, it's been taking up more and more of my time." Mrs. Wakefield put her arms around her daughters. "Now I know it's going to have to stay part-time. Because, Frank, I think you'll agree that raising three children is definitely a full-time job."

Mr. Howard grinned and nodded. "I'm going to miss your artistic touch, but I understand."

"So it looks like we're just one big happy family again," Mr. Wakefield concluded. "And I'd just like to say one more thing."

"What's that?" Steven asked. The twins looked up expectantly.

"I'm starved." Mr. Wakefield clapped his hands together. "If we hurry, I'm sure we'll be able to find a table at DeSalvio's. Of course, you kids will have to get cleaned up a bit first." He turned to Mr. Howard and his fiancée. "We'd love it if you two would join us."

"Yes, please do," Elizabeth said happily. "It'll be our way of making it up to you."

"I promise not to add any of my special dressing to your salad," Jessica promised, holding up her hand solemnly.

"My eyes water just thinking about it," Mr. Howard joked.

The twins and Steven quickly ran upstairs to change their clothes and wash up. When they came back down, they all put on their coats and moved to the front door.

"I think you and Frank will like this little restaurant," Mrs. Wakefield said to Karen. "It's so romantic. Ned and I went there on our first date."

Elizabeth's ears perked up. "Your very first date?"

"Yes," Mrs. Wakefield replied. "I've been meaning to tell you."

Elizabeth could hardly contain her excitement. Finally she'd be able to finish her interview. "Let me get my notepad and pen."

"It's really pretty silly," Mr. Wakefield said, chuckling. "Let's get in the van and we'll tell you all about it on the way over."

"Why don't we take the limousine?" Mr. Howard cut in. "There's plenty of room."

"Could we drive by the Dairi Burger?" Jessica asked excitedly. She was sure some of the Unicorns would be there and this would really impress them.

Mr. Howard nodded and the children raced for the front door.

"A silver limo. This is all right!" Steven shouted as the sleek car pulled away and headed toward the heart of Sweet Valley.

When they got home that evening, Elizabeth could hardly wait to call Amy. She raced to the telephone in the hall, and quickly dialed Amy's number, then carried the phone with its long cord into her bedroom.

"Elizabeth!" Amy shrieked into the receiver the minute she picked up the phone. "I've been sitting here all night, waiting for you to call. Boy, your dad sure looked angry."

"Sorry," Elizabeth apologized, "but I never got a chance to call. After we explained the whole mess to everyone, my dad took us all out to dinner. But here's the *best* news! I found out how Mom and Dad first met."

"Oooh, great! Tell me everything."

"Well, it was seventeen years ago," Elizabeth began. "Dad was in law school and Mom had just finished college and was working as a waitress while she was looking for a job in the design field."

"Where?"

"At DeSalvio's, the restaurant we went to tonight. She only worked there a short time because she found a job decorating windows at Morgan's. But anyway, it was close to graduation and Dad and his three roommates had reserved a table to celebrate. Each one of them had a date."

"Was your mom your dad's date?"

"No, she was his waitress."

"What! Your dad was out with someone else?"

"Amy, if you'll just listen, I'll tell you how they met. You see, this was Mom's first night as a waitress. She was really nervous to have a table of eight to serve."

"Especially if one of them is a handsome man like your dad."

Elizabeth giggled. "That's exactly what Mom said. So, anyway, she put all of the food on one of those big silver trays and—"

"Oh, no!" Amy broke in. "Did she spill it?"

"Yes, all over Dad! Spaghetti, lasagna, and eggplant, with tons of tomato sauce."

"Oooh, how awful!"

"Mom said she was never so embarrassed in her life," Elizabeth continued. "She ran back into the kitchen and cried and cried."

"What did your dad do?" Amy asked. "Was he mad?"

"No, he said it was so awful that it was funny. There he was with his clothes all ruined, the entire table's dinner on the floor, and his date mad at him for laughing about it."

"And then what happened?"

"Chef DeSalvio had Dad go into the kitchen and put on a pair of white pants and a shirt while he cleaned his clothes."

"That's where he found your mom?"

"Yes, and Mom said he looked really cute in the chef's outfit. He sat down and the two of them started talking—"

"And he forgot all about his other date," Amy jumped in. "He only had eyes for your mom."

"Right. Then Chef DeSalvio came in and told Dad that the restaurant owed him a full dinner. Dad's date and his friends had left so he invited Mom to join him. The chef set up a little table with candles on it in the kitchen, and they fell in love while the chef's brother, Tony, serenaded them with his mandolin."

"How romantic!"

"Isn't it?" Elizabeth said dreamily. "After they told us that story, Jessica made them promise to go back to DeSalvio's every year on their anniversary."

"Do you think they'll do it?" Amy asked.

"Well, if I know Jessica, next year she'll have arranged for their anniversary dinner to be served in the kitchen with Tony serenading them. She'll probably even find a way to have Dad wear a chef's outfit."

Jessica, who was just about to knock on her sister's door, overheard Elizabeth's comment and smiled to herself. *What a great idea!*

She went back to her room and as she hopped into bed, she thought, *I'll get started on it right away. Next year's anniversary will be the best one ever!*

Twelve

◇

"Jessica! Over here, quick!" Elizabeth called across the noisy lunchroom.

"We did it!" Amy Sutton shouted out. "We got an—"

"Amy!" Elizabeth gave her friend a gentle shove. "I think I should be the one to tell my sister the good news."

"Good news?" Jessica slid into an empty seat. "What is it?"

"Our Living History project," Pamela Jacobson explained.

"Mrs. Arnette gave us an A on it," Elizabeth said happily.

"Lizzie, that's great!" Jessica gave her sister a hug. "You deserved it."

Elizabeth smiled. "I think that was the hardest report I've ever done."

"You know something?" Amy broke in. "I think that is the first A I've ever gotten from the Hairnet. This really calls for a celebration. Like an extra piece of peach cobbler." She looked hungrily at Pamela's plate. "Who's not going to eat hers?"

"No, you don't!" Pamela snatched up her plate to keep it away from Amy. But it was too late.

"Amy!" Pamela squealed. "Give it back."

"It's mine, all mine!" Amy chortled.

Elizabeth and Jessica laughed as Pamela struggled to get back the cobbler. Suddenly the cobbler flew off the plate. The girls watched the sticky dessert sail through the air and land in a gloppy mess at the feet of a girl walking by.

It was Billie Layton, one of the best athletes in the sixth grade and an ace pitcher on the neighborhood Little League team. Her real name was Belinda but everyone called her Billie.

"Watch what you're doing!" Billie snapped. "I could've stepped in that."

"Sorry, Billie," Amy giggled. "We were just joking around."

"Great!" Billie checked her sneakers to see if any of the sticky dessert had gotten on them. "Next time keep your jokes to yourself."

Amy looked stunned. "I said I was sorry."

Billie didn't say any more but turned and marched out of the lunchroom.

"What's the matter with her?" Jessica asked after Amy had wiped the dessert off the floor with a napkin and tossed it in the trash.

"I don't know," Pamela said. "She's usually so nice."

Amy shook her head. "Something must be wrong. I heard Billie caused a scene in baseball practice yesterday."

"What?" Elizabeth exclaimed. "She's always so easygoing."

"She struck out," Amy continued. "She got so mad, she threw her bat over the fence."

"Who told you?" Pamela asked.

"Jim Sturbridge," Amy replied. "He's the catcher. Jim told me that the coach made her go straight home."

"She's sure acting weird," Elizabeth whispered. "She didn't even look like herself just now."

"Well, if I was the only girl on a team full of boys," Jessica said, "I guess I'd act funny, too."

"Maybe she's doing badly in school," Amy suggested.

"I don't think so," Elizabeth answered. "She got a hundred on that big math test last week."

"Did you know her mom works in the library?" Pamela said.

"You mean, that pregnant lady?" Jessica asked.

Pamela nodded. "Maybe that has something to do with it."

"Oh, I doubt it. It would be really neat to have a baby sister or brother," Elizabeth said.

"Unless the baby turned into another Steven," Jessica cracked. They all laughed and the subject soon changed to other school gossip.

As they left the cafeteria to go to class, Elizabeth noticed Billie leaning against a row of lockers, staring at the floor. She looked so sad, Elizabeth's heart went out to her.

Well, Elizabeth thought to herself. *If I can find out what's bothering her, maybe I can help her.*

What's wrong with Billie Layton? Find out in *Sweet Valley Twins* #25, STANDING OUT.

Join Jessica and Elizabeth for another exciting adventure in *Sweet Valley Twins* Super Edition #2, HOLIDAY MISCHIEF.

YOUR OWN

SWEET VALLEY HIGH

SLAM BOOK!

If you've read *Slambook Fever*, Sweet Valley High #48, you know that slam books are the rage at Sweet Valley High. Now *you* can have a slam book of your own! Make up your own categories, such as "Biggest Jock" or "Best Looking," and have your friends fill in the rest! There's a four-page calendar, horoscopes and questions most asked by Sweet Valley readers with answers from Elizabeth and Jessica

It's a must for SWEET VALLEY fans!

☐ 05496 FRANCINE PASCAL'S SWEET VALLEY HIGH
      SLAM BOOK
      Laurie Pascal Wenk $3.50

- -

THE CLASS TRIP

SWEET VALLEY TWINS SUPER EDITION #1

Join Jessica and Elizabeth in the very first SWEET VALLEY TWINS Super Edition—it's longer, can be read out of sequence, and is full of page-turning excitement!

The day of the big sixth-grade class trip to the Enchanted Forest is finally here! But Jessica and Elizabeth have a fight and spend the beginning of the trip arguing. When Elizabeth decides to make up, Jessica has disappeared. In a frantic search for her sister, Elizabeth finds herself in a series of dangerous and exciting Alice In Wonderland-type of adventures.

☐ 15588-1 $2.95/$3.50 in Canada

Buy them at your local bookstore or use this page to order.

Special Offer
Buy a Bantam Book
for only 50¢.

Now you can order the exciting books you've been wanting to read straight from Bantam's latest catalog of hundreds of titles. *And* this special offer gives you the opportunity to purchase a Bantam book for only 50¢. Here's how:

By ordering any five books at the regular price per order, you can also choose any other single book listed (up to a $5.95 value) for only 50¢. Some restrictions do apply, so for further details send for Bantam's catalog of titles today.

Just send us your name and address and we'll send you Bantam Book's SHOP AT HOME CATALOG!